START YOUR ENGINES!

SPORTS CARS

By Emma Huddleston

Kaleidoscope
Minneapolis, MN

The Quest for Discovery Never Ends

This edition first published in 2020 by Kaleidoscope Publishing, Inc.

For information regarding permission, write to
Kaleidoscope Publishing, Inc.
6012 Blue Circle Drive
Minnetonka, MN 55343

Library of Congress Control Number
2019940183

ISBN
978-1-64519-061-5 (library bound)
978-1-64494-219-2 (paperback)
978-1-64519-162-9 (ebook)

Printed in the United States of America.

Bigfoot lurks within one of the images in this book. It's up to you to find him!

TABLE OF CONTENTS

Chapter 1: Extraordinary Speed 4

Chapter 2: History of Sports Cars 10

Chapter 3: High Performance 16

Chapter 4: Amateur and Professional 22

Beyond the Book 28

Research Ninja 29

Further Resources 30

Glossary 31

Index 32

Photo Credits 32

About the Author 32

CHAPTER 1

Extraordinary Speed

Vrrrrrrooomm! Troy speeds off down the road. He's in his sleek new Mazda MX-5 Miata sports car. He has the roof down. The evening breeze ruffles his hair. The sky darkens. His car's shiny black paint blends in. Headlights light up the pavement. Troy smiles. He loves the feel of this new car.

Sports cars are slightly different from everyday cars. They're sleeker. They usually only seat two people. Their engines are more powerful. Sports cars can go faster than regular cars. They're even used for racing. Some car companies make sports cars with **V8** engines. This puts the power of race cars into a car you can drive on the street.

The Mazda MX-5 Miata is a convertible. This means that the top of the car opens up.

Troy turns around a sharp corner. The Miata has rear-wheel drive. Many sports cars have this feature. It helps the car's **handling**. It lets the car grip the road better when it **accelerates**. And rear-wheel drive evens out the weight of the car.

Troy presses the gas pedal. He speeds up out of the turn. His car reaches high speeds quickly. Sometimes high speeds make normal car rides feel bumpy. Driving a sports car feels smooth. Troy's Miata has great **suspension**. He isn't jolted up and down.

Sports cars can travel on highways and city streets.

Troy veers around another corner. It's getting late. He turns his Miata onto the highway. He'll take the long way home.

SPORTS CARS VS. FORMULA ONE CARS

Sports cars and Formula One (F1) race cars are both sleek. They're both built to go fast. But they don't have much else in common. F1 race cars have single seats and an open top. They have a narrow shape with a wing on the back. Sports cars usually have two seats. They might have convertible tops or regular roofs.

F1 race cars are only for racing. Sports cars can be driven on ordinary roads.

HOW BIG IS A SPORTS CAR?

FUN FACT

One definition for a sports car is a small two-door car made for speed and handling.

Width
68 inches
(173 cm)

SEDAN

Width
72 inches (183 cm)

Length
104 inches (264 cm)

SPORTS CAR

Height
49 inches
(124 cm)
Length
91 inches (231 cm)
Height
58 inches
(147 cm)

CHAPTER 2

History of Sports Cars

In the early 1900s, cars were still new. People started racing. These race cars were some of the first sports cars. Newspapers wrote about the races. People read the stories. They would buy the models that won first place.

Some races in the early 1900s took place on the sand at Daytona Beach in Florida.

FUN FACT

By 1900, cars reached speeds of about 50 miles per hour (80 km/h) during races.

Races made sports cars more popular. They spurred new developments. Over time, sports cars became their own category of cars.

Max Hoffman sold cars in the 1940s. Sports cars were becoming popular. But not many models were available in the United States. The best models were made in Europe. He decided to take a risk. He opened his own store in New York in 1946. He sold cars that came from Europe.

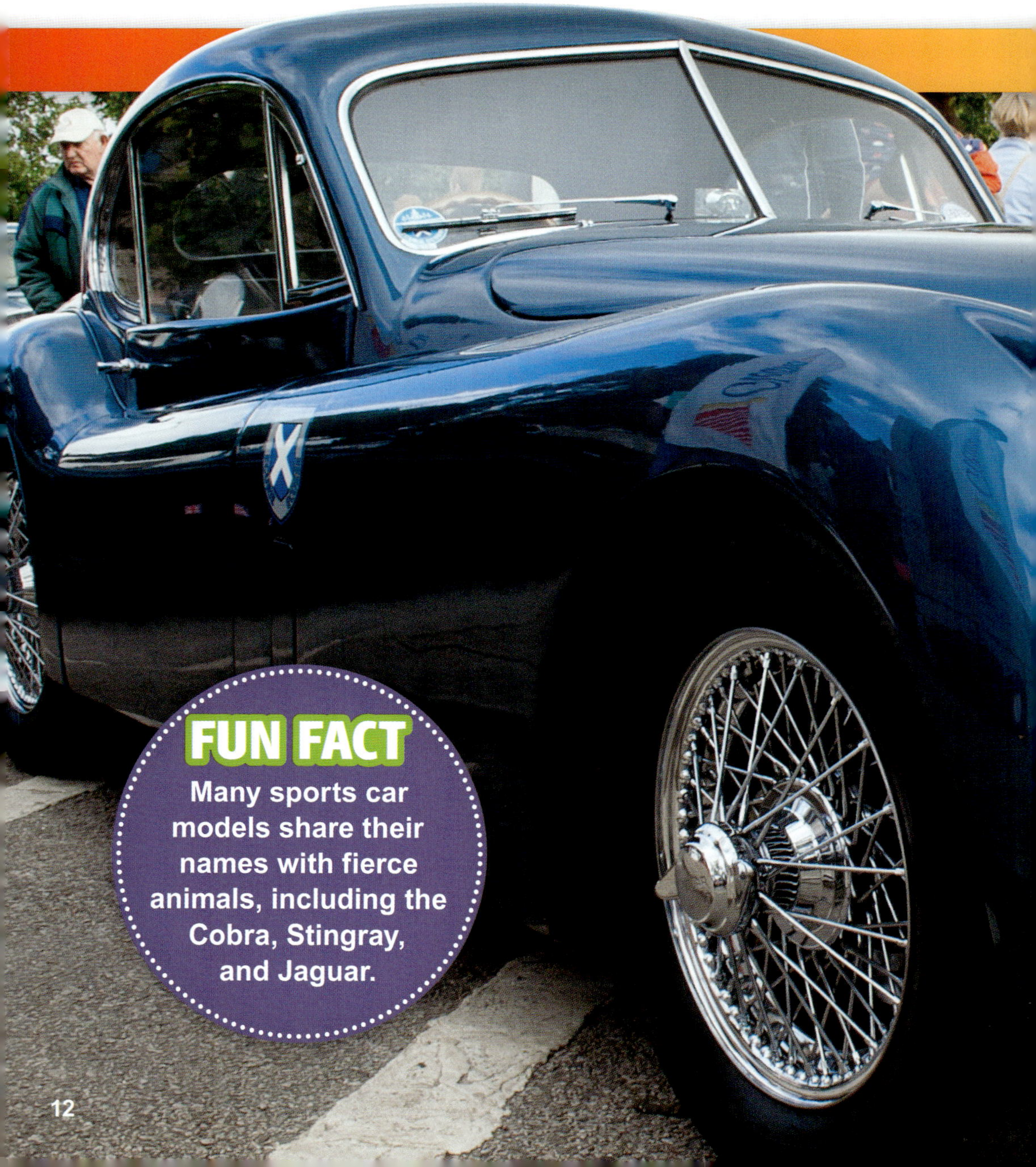

FUN FACT

Many sports car models share their names with fierce animals, including the Cobra, Stingray, and Jaguar.

At first, he only sold expensive French Delahaye cars. But soon, he carried Jaguars and MGs. He sold sports cars for 25 years. He introduced the United States to many foreign brands. He was one of the first to sell Porsches. Hoffman helped increase American interest in foreign cars.

The Jaguar XK120 was a sports car that was produced during the 1940s and 1950s.

Some people today still drive sports cars made in the 1950s.

Leon puts on his reading glasses. He subscribes to a magazine about sports cars. This issue has an article about the newest Ferrari. It takes him back to his younger years. He watched a bright red Ferrari race in 1953. It won the first World Sportscar Championship. Ferrari cars won for many years after that. Sports cars became extremely popular in the 1950s. Companies made new models. Some cost up to $50,000. That would be almost $500,000 today. That's enough to buy a house!

Leon remembers when the Thunderbird came out in 1955. Ford made it. It was red. It had a convertible top. People enjoyed cruising around town in it. Leon got one. He even entered some races in it. His racing days are over. But he still drives sports cars for fun.

CHAPTER 3

High Performance

Anna lives in Switzerland. She and her mom went to the 2019 Geneva Motor Show. They looked at the cars. Companies displayed shiny new models. One caught her eye. It was bright green. Its black hood had an orange stripe down the middle. It was the TECHART GTstreet RS. It's a custom-built sports car. TECHART modifies cars, which means it changes the cars from the original models. The GTstreet RS is based on the Porsche 911 Turbo S.

Anna was making a video to show her dad. He had to miss the auto show. But he loved sports cars. She zoomed in on the wheels with her camera. The rims had aero rings. These pieces covered spaces between the **spokes**. They protected the brake system and wheels. They prevented damage from strong winds and pebbles on the roads.

Many people attend the Geneva Motor Show each year. They can view the latest sports cars.

FUN FACT

Many sports cars use massive air-powered brakes to stop.

All Porsche 911 models have rear engines.

The GTstreet RS's engine was at the back of the car. Anna thought that was really cool. TECHART changed the Porsche engine. It added 180 extra horsepower. And it added **torque**. This helped the car accelerate quickly. It could go from 0 to 62 miles per hour (100 km/h) in just 2.5 seconds. Anna's family had a regular Toyota Camry. It took 8.2 seconds to reach that speed. TECHART's changes didn't add any weight. This kept the car light and fast. It could go 211 miles per hour (340 km/h).

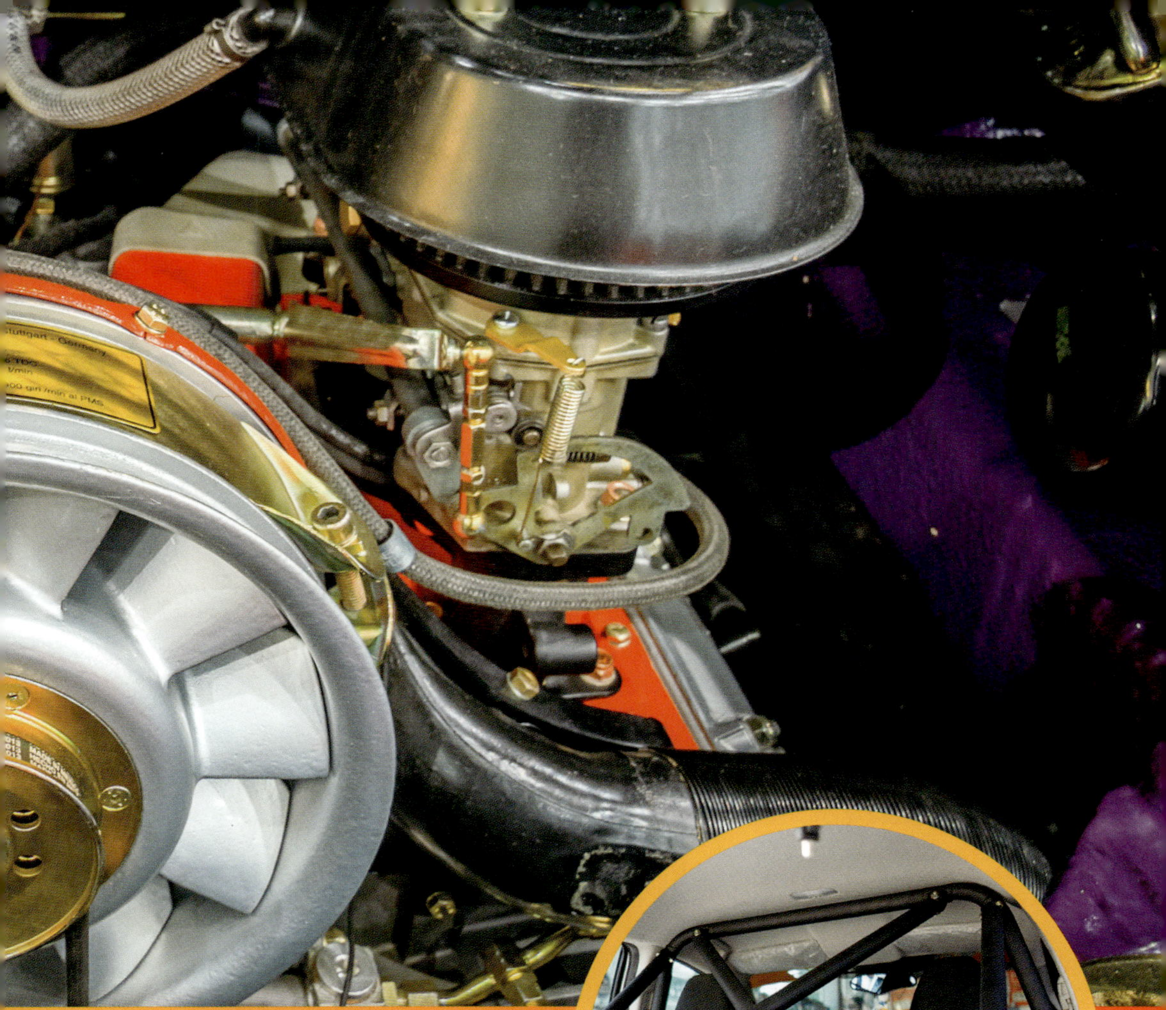

Anna looked inside the car. Black leather and wool covered the driver's seat. It had a harness with six straps instead of a seatbelt. There wasn't a door handle—just a simple orange strap. A roll cage sat behind the seats. It was an orange metal frame. It would protect passengers in a serious crash.

Spoilers help keep sports cars from flipping over when they reach top speeds.

Anna stepped back. She fit the whole car in her camera's frame. The car's design was **aerodynamic**. The front was round and low. Wings and fins on the car directed airflow. The spoiler stuck up in the back. It moved air around the car to decrease **drag**. The spoiler also kept the back of the car pressed down. It prevented wind from flipping the car.

Anna walked around the car with her camera. She got every last detail. The GTstreet RS was rare. Only ten were being made. She knew her dad would love it.

SPORTS CAR

STATS

MODEL	HORSEPOWER
Porsche 911 Turbo S	580 horsepower
TOP SPEED	**WEIGHT**
205 miles per hour (330 km/h)	3,528 pounds (1,600 kg)
BASE PRICE	**SPECIAL FEATURES**
$190,700	Rear-located engine, rear-axle steering, 20-inch (50 cm) wheels

CHAPTER 4

Amateur and Professional

Sports cars are used in many types of competitions. Addie sits in her BMW M6 GT3. She tries to shake her nerves. It's race day. Addie is an **amateur**. Most sports car races are for amateur drivers.

Addie used to race her everyday sports car. She entered timed competitions. She drove courses on her own. Other racers would do the same. The racer with the fastest time would win. But now she enters tougher competitions. She goes neck-and-neck with other racers. She bought this BMW for racing.

Amateur and professional racers around the world drive the BMW M6 GT3.

ZOOM IN ON A

SPORTS CAR

Addie drives in regional races. Her goal is to make it to the GT Daytona class. It's part of the International Motor Sports Association (IMSA) SportsCar Championship. Professionals and amateurs race together in that class. They drive cars that are sold race ready. The engines all generate about 500 horsepower. Addie looks at the other drivers. She takes a deep breath. She knows she can win. Soon, she'll be racing with the pros.

FUN FACT
Some races are only for vintage sports car models.

Sports car races can take place in all weather conditions.

Fernando Alonso is in the driver's seat. He drives a Toyota TSO50 Hybrid. He hasn't gotten much rest. But he has to focus. He's racing in the 24 Hours of Le Mans. It is the ultimate endurance race for sports cars. An endurance race takes place over a long time or distance to test athletes' abilities. The race is held in France. It began in 1923. The car that travels farthest in 24 hours wins.

The track is 8.5 miles (13.6 km) long. Cars reach speeds over 200 miles per hour (321 km/h). Alonso and his team make lap after lap. Groups of three people drive. They switch every 1.5 to 2 hours. The race is tough. It tests the car and the drivers.

Drivers must use safety features such as headlights during long endurance races.

Alonso presses his foot to the gas. Trees blur outside the window. Soon, the 24 hours are up. Alonso's team wins! They made 388 laps. Their Toyota TSO50 Hybrid was a winner.

Smooth, sleek sports cars are popular vehicles. Some zip around racetracks. Others drive on regular roads. No matter how they're used, sports cars highlight the best part of racing: speed.

BEYOND THE BOOK

After reading the book, it's time to think about what you learned. Try the following exercises to jumpstart your ideas.

THINK

THAT'S NEWS TO ME. Many companies put cars on display at the Geneva Motor Show. Consider how news sources might be able to fill in more detail on this event. What new information could be found in news articles? Where could you go to find those news sources?

CREATE

PRIMARY SOURCES. Primary sources provide firsthand accounts of an event. Primary sources can include interviews, videos, or photographs. Make a list of primary sources you might be able to find on sports cars.

SHARE

WHAT'S YOUR OPINION? The text states that some sports cars put the power of racing into normal cars. Do you agree? Provide evidence from the text to support your position. Then share your position and evidence with a friend. Does your friend find your argument convincing?

GROW

DRAWING CONNECTIONS. Create a diagram that shows and explains connections between sports cars and professional racing. How does learning about professional racing help you to better understand sports cars?

RESEARCH NINJA

Visit www.ninjaresearcher.com/0615 to learn how to take your research skills and book report writing to the next level!

RESEARCH

DIGITAL LITERACY TOOLS

SEARCH LIKE A PRO
Learn about how to use search engines to find useful websites.

FACT OR FAKE?
Discover how you can tell a trusted website from an untrustworthy resource.

TEXT DETECTIVE
Explore how to zero in on the information you need most.

SHOW YOUR WORK
Research responsibly—learn how to cite sources.

WRITE

GET TO THE POINT
Learn how to express your main ideas.

PLAN OF ATTACK
Learn prewriting exercises and create an outline.

DOWNLOADABLE REPORT FORMS

Further Resources

BOOKS

Fishman, Jon. *Cool Sports Cars*. Lerner Publications, 2019.

Lanier, Wendy Hinote. *Sports Cars*. Focus Readers, 2017.

Willson, Quentin. *Cool Cars*. DK Publishing, 2014.

WEBSITES

FACTSURFER

Factsurfer.com gives you a safe, fun way to find more information.

1. Go to www.factsurfer.com.
2. Enter "Sports Cars" into the search box and click 🔍.
3. Select your book cover to see a list of related websites.

Glossary

accelerate: To accelerate is to gain speed. Sports car engines can accelerate quickly to high speeds.

aerodynamic: Something is aerodynamic if it moves easily and smoothly through air. Sports cars have smooth designs and features like spoilers to help make them more aerodynamic.

amateur: An amateur is a person who isn't paid to participate in an activity, especially a sport. Addie competes against other amateurs, but she hopes to race with professionals one day.

drag: Drag is the force of air resistance on a vehicle. Sports cars have very little drag.

handling: Handling is how well a vehicle responds to what the driver does behind the wheel. Sports cars often have great handling.

spokes: Spokes are thin metal bars that connect the center of a wheel and its edge. The spokes help protect the wheel.

suspension: The suspension is part of a metal car frame that connects the wheels to the body of the car. Riding in the Audi RS 5 Sportback felt smooth because the suspension moved up and down over rough ground.

torque: In a vehicle engine, torque is a force that turns the wheels. The GTstreet RS had added torque, which helped improve its acceleration speed.

V8: A V8 engine is a large engine with eight cylinders that are arranged in the shape of a V. Many sports cars have V8 engines because they are powerful.

Index

24 Hours of Le Mans, 26

Alonso, Fernando, 26–27
amateurs, 22, 25

BMW M6 GT3, 22–23

Delahaye, 13

engines, 4, 18, 21, 25

Ferrari, 15
Ford, 15
Formula One (F1), 7

Geneva Motor Show, 16
GTstreet RS, 16–20

Hoffman, Max, 12–13
horsepower, 18, 21, 25

Jaguar, 13

Mazda, 4–7
MGs, 13

Porsche, 13, 16–18, 21
professionals, 25

TECHART, 16–18
Toyota, 18, 26–27

wing, 7, 20
World Sportscar Championship, 15

PHOTO CREDITS

The images in this book are reproduced through the courtesy of: Porsche Media Center, front cover (car); Orientaly/Shutterstock Images, front cover (road); Dan74/Shutterstock Images, pp. 3, 22, 22–23; emirhankaramuk/Shutterstock Images, pp. 4–5, 8–9 (sports car); mevans/iStockphoto, p. 6; Natursports/Shutterstock Images, p. 7; nitinut380/Shutterstock Images, pp. 8–9 (sedan); AP Images, pp. 10–11; johnbraid/Shutterstock Images, pp. 12–13; iShootPhotosLLC/iStockphoto, pp. 14–15; benedek/iStockphoto, p. 15; Mustafa Yalcin/Anadolu Agency/Getty Images, pp. 16–17; Daniel Pullen/Future Publishing/Getty Images, pp. 18–19; Sista Vongjintanaruks/Shutterstock Images, p. 19; Kaukola Photography/Shutterstock Images, p. 20; Red Line Editorial, pp. 21 (chart); Tlpixs/Shutterstock Images, p. 21 (car); Dan74/Shutterstock Images, p. 24; Thanninsri/Shutterstock Images, p. 25; Jean-Francois Monier/AFP/Getty Images, pp. 26–27; Loic Venance/AFP/Getty Images, p. 27; Thanakrit Sathavornmanee/Shutterstock Images, p. 30.

ABOUT THE AUTHOR

Emma Huddleston enjoys reading and swing dancing. She lives in the Twin Cities with her husband.